Dedication

To Scott and James
for insisting upon
"Daddy's Imagination Stories"
for bedtime storytelling.

Note of Thanks

Thanks to my editors Alexandra Petropoulos and Eleanor Smith for their guidance and terrific attention to detail. Chris Hammond for the overall book design, publishing advice and his digital wizardry enhancing the artwork.

With special thanks to Alan Titshall for his notes on the first draft, encouragement and relentless enthusiasm. To my darling wife Nicola Bunce for taking the time out from creating her coveted willow sculptures to provide the original watercolour artwork and for her unwavering support to bring these adventures to life.

The Secret Adventures of Franacken Petalblower and Friends
By G. J. Bunce

ISBN 978-1-3999-3436-7 paperback
Copyright © 2022 Gary John Bunce
All rights reserved
First Edition

The Secret Adventures of
Franacken Petalblower
and Friends

G. J. Bunce

Arden Publishing
c/o IBB Law LLP
Capital Court
30 Windsor Street
Uxbridge
Middlesex
UB8 1AB
ENGLAND

gjbunceauthor@gmail.com

Before Colour

N ow, first things first. Before I can tell you about any of the little folk who live in the world called *Outside*, I need you to look closely at your thumb. Try very hard to imagine a little person who is no bigger than half of your thumb, with long spiky hair coloured yellow, green, red and brown. You are nearly there, but not quite. This little person is dressed in green pyjamas, a green cape, and a pair of yellow boots. Got it? Finally, imagine your tiny new friend holding a tiny paintbrush which, to fit their tiny little hand, will be only half the size of your eyelash. Now, let's see how you have done.

"BOO!
HOW ARE YOU?
My name is
FRANACKEN
PETALBLOWER
and I really love
colours and painting.
DO YOU?"

How old do you think he is? Well, Franacken Petalblower is 346 years old and so is still very young by little folk standards who can live for 2,000 years, give or take a century.

Franacken says he is an artist, but between you and me, he is not a very good one. Don't tell him I said that, because he thinks he is the best artist that has ever lived – ever!

He certainly loved to paint and he used to paint absolutely anything. But when I say paint, I don't mean the way that perhaps you would paint a picture of your pet cat or dog on white paper. No, Franacken actually painted on the dog, cat, hamster, or any other creature he could catch. The animals did not seem to mind being painted as the brushes tickled and the paint smelt like scrumptious marmalade.

Unsurprisingly, the people who own the animals were very cross indeed to find their pet painted from head to paw, paw to tail. So, the more creatures Franacken painted, the more he got into trouble with the Elders, who are a bit like the head teachers at your school. But Franacken did not care and would not listen. In fact, once he even painted Casperoon Eartheater (the eldest of the Elders) whilst Casperoon told him off! It is very hard to tell someone off when you are being tickled by brushes that make you giggle! Naughty Franacken!

Anyway, where was I? Oh yes, back to the story. So... Once upon a day, and a very busy day it was too, Franacken had managed to paint five dogs, three cats, two snakes, four birds, two frogs (when they stopped jumping about!!), and half of a sheep (he gave up on the sheep after his brushes got tangled and stuck in the wool). The Elders, needless to say, were furious and Franacken was officially in the **deepest** of quadruple trouble. All the Elders and everyone from the world of *Outside* came to see Franacken stand upon the Naughty Step, which is a rather large, very old, damp tree stump covered in moss. Everyone was super cross and stared at the lonely figure of Franacken Petalblower, who stood all by himself.

There was absolute silence as Casperoon Eartheater approached the young artist. Even the noisy woodpecker stopped pecking to see what would happen to Franacken this time.

"Young Petalblower," bellowed Casperoon, "the Elders have decided that you are to give me all your paintbrushes."

Phew, thought Franacken, *is that all? No problem!*

"AND," Casperoon continued, *"YOU MUST NEVER EVER, EVER, TIMES A THOUSAND, PAINT AGAIN!"*

"Never paint again?" Franacken whimpered. His bottom lip moved, then it trembled, and then he cried like he had never cried before. He cried so much that a passing ant had to pop open his umbrella. Poor Franacken!

"NEVER EVER PAINT AGAIN," the other Elders repeated. So, punishment had been passed and the Elders seemed very pleased with their decision, even though Franacken had cried so much that the whole of the tree stump was now soaked with his tears. Poor Franacken. He was so sad. But then... someone approached.

"Wait a minute!" snapped an old woman from the crowd. "Casperoon, you are being far too hard on the boy."

Casperoon recognised his wife's voice immediately and tried to ignore her, which was not a good idea as Winceyfloss, his wife, was also a witch and she was rather a good one at that. She often practised her magic on her poor husband. Only last week she had turned him into a slug, then a pig and a fish in a jar just for fun. Casperoon had just remembered this fact and decided he had better be very nice to his wife.

He turned to face her with a big smile and said ever so sweetly, "My darling Wincey Woo Woo, how good of you to turn up to a meeting of the Elders, but I am afraid, my dear, that the punishment has been passed. So... erm... sorry?"

"Poppledosh!" snorted Wincey Woo Woo... erm... I mean Winceyfloss. "The boy," she continued, "should be allowed to paint, but I agree Franacken should not be allowed to paint whatever he wants – especially animals. If we put his talents to good use, it could brighten up the place. The world *Outside* certainly needs some colour. I say he must never ever paint anything but..." There was a hush. "But, hmm. Let me see." The old witch looked around and then exclaimed, "He can paint the leaves on the trees!"

There were audible gasps. Paint the leaves? Still, who would argue with a witch? Even a good or mostly good witch. "Now I say that's decided then – agreed? Or shall I turn you all into slugs for a day?" Everyone quickly nodded in agreement – I mean, slugs are a bit slimy.

Winceyfloss had a good reason for her idea. She never liked the leaves in the world of *Outside.* They never changed colour and were always, well, greyish. Grey in spring, summer, autumn, and winter. Always and forever, dreary grey. Nobody likes grey really, especially old witches – although black is another matter, of course. Black is simply a must for hats, cats, and flip-flops.

The Elders huddled and muttered amongst themselves. They looked over at the witch occasionally, who was staring at them by now and clearly growing a little impatient as she awaited their response. The fact was that although the Elders were allowed to make everyday decisions, the old witch often interfered with the big, difficult decisions, so this was not a surprise. The other fact was none of the Elders wanted to be turned into a slug. So, the Elders agreed that the leaves on the trees could be painted and Casperoon returned the paintbrushes to the young artist on this strict understanding.

"Just the leaves, young Franacken. ***JUST THE LEAVES***!"

Franacken was so excited that he jumped with joy from the tree stump to the nearest tree and started painting immediately. Unfortunately, the nearest tree was the Elders' Most Sacred and Holy Ancient Tree. Before the Elders could say "Somebody stop him!" Franacken had painted half the leaves the brightest of yellows. Poor, sad Elders. What had they agreed to?

The Elders huddled together and cried liked they had never cried before. Now all the ants had to pop up their umbrellas. Of all the hundreds of trees to be painted, the young artist had chosen their precious sacred tree. They did not think he would dream of painting this special tree. They were so very sad. But then, after a while, a strange thing happened. Casperoon, mid-sob, looked up at their sacred tree and then, slowly, he walked towards it. The leaves were actually quite beautiful. Gradually, everyone, including the other Elders, were amazed by the new, wonderful colours.

Franacken painted the very last leaf at the tip-top of the tree and then he jumped into the air, did a double somersault, opened his rather large cape and glided safely and slowly to the ground. As he floated down, he stroked his chin and admired his work. He was extremely pleased with himself. By the time he landed, he was blushing the brightest of red as everybody was now cheering and clapping.

"Hooray for Franacken! Hooray for the Leaf Painter."

Franacken felt like the best artist that had ever lived. And to be fair, he is rather good at painting leaves. Even better, the Elders were so happy that they decided that every single tree in the world known as *Outside* should be painted more often to celebrate the four seasons of the year. They would be painted fresh salad green in the spring, warm green and blossom pink in the summer, reds, yellows, and golds in autumn, and dark chocolate brown in the winter. The Elders decreed that as there were so many leaves, everyone from that day forth should become a *Leaf Painter* to get the job done. After all, it was a huge job to do.

There was a slight panic when the leaves fell off in winter, which they never did when they were dreary grey. The tiny twigs that held the leaves were not used to holding a heavy leaf coated in four layers of paint. Poor twigs.

To the Elders' relief, the leaves grew back again in the spring, albeit a dreary grey. Everyone cheered when the leaves returned, and they promptly painted them again in just one day. If the truth were known (and trees always tell the truth), the trees did not really like boring old grey either. The trees also appreciated all the extra attention they received by thousands of little folk flying about with their flapping capes, painting their leaves in exciting colours and... they liked the way the brushes tickled!!

From then on, the little folk officially became known as the *Leaf Painters*, which was much better than simply being known as, well, just little folk who wear capes.

Franacken is still painting today, and he may be outside your window right now painting a tree. Can you see him? It is not easy. After all, he is very small, as you now know, and his green cape looks like... go on, guess! Yes, that's right – a leaf!

Nearly the End

So now you know why the leaves change colour in the world of *Outside*. But please do not paint leaves. After all, it is not your job and it may upset the *Leaf Painters*, which is not a good idea. You may find that an upset *Leaf Painter* might paint your pet cat, dog, hamster, fish, or even you with purple paint, which is Franacken's favourite colour at the moment. But do come and visit them sometime. You can find their home on the secret map. Good luck with spotting Franacken as he whizzes about quicker than a blink!

Really the End... of this adventure.
Do join the Leaf Painters again on the next one!

The Most Fantastical Games

Time to meet our unlikeliest of heroes, Totalee Tomtum.
"Yo Yippy Hum! I'M TOTALEE TOMTUM."

Believe it or not, if it were not for this little chap, the *Leaf Painters'* Most Fantastical Olympic Games would never have existed. More of that a tiny bit later, but have you noticed Totalee is wearing a cap? *Leaf Painters* never wear caps as a rule, or hats, or even scarves, as they like their colourful spiky hair to be seen by absolutely everyone – including the trees that instantly recognise their little friends who tickle their leaves with paintbrushes. Well, the fact is, Totalee has always been a little different, ever since he was a young boy of 187 years old. His mother, Twinkly Tomtum, always had problems with her little boy. He never seemed to enjoy Leaf

Painting like, well, everyone else. Instead, he would disappear every morning and not come back until buttercup teatime. Twinkly worried about Totalee a lot, as mothers do, but she could see her little boy was the happiest when he went off for his adventures, which certainly and absolutely did NOT involve painting leaves... not even a tiny one!

Totalee had his most exciting adventure at a place that does not sound very exciting at all. Boring Snoring Land. You see, I told you, a very unexciting name for any place indeed. But this land would change Totalee's life forever – all of the *Leaf Painters'* lives, for that matter.

Boring Snoring Land was so named because there were hardly any trees at all. Instead, there were mainly hills, streams, and very good paths that were designed to get you out of Boring Snoring Land as quickly as possible should you find yourself there by mistake. The fact is, there is not one leaf to be painted in Boring Snoring Land, so you can see why this place was of no interest to the *Leaf Painters*. But it was Totalee's playground, and he loved it.

Totalee discovered his beloved Boring Snoring Land as a result of a happy accident, which is far better than an unhappy accident!

Once upon a long afternoon, and it was a very long and dull afternoon as far as Totalee was concerned, he and his mother were having to paint the leaves dark chocolate brown with all the other *Leaf Painters* to celebrate the beginning of winter.

Everyone was so happy and sang as they painted, mainly because they loved the way dark chocolate brown paint smelt. Not like chocolate, but scrumptious marmalade, of course. Almost everyone was singing, but not Totalee. He hated painting leaves and was only there because Twinkly had said he would be sent to the Elders if he did not join in. So, as he was trying to be a good little boy that day, he painted. But he did not sing and he also left his cape at home completely on purpose. AND he covered his lovely spiky hair with his cap, so he was not wearing a proper *Leaf Painter* costume at all and did not care – not one bit. SO THERE! Needless to say, everyone (including the trees) thought he looked a little out of place.

Twinkly blushed red with embarrassment.

But then the very *happy* accident happened. Scruffy McQuinn,
quite a naughty little boy, painted the twig where Totalee was standing.

No, he had not missed the leaf by mistake; he had painted the twig absolutely on purpose because he knew that dark chocolate brown paint was the most slippery of all the paints. You can guess what happened next, can't you? Poor Totalee slipped, then double-flipped and fell. And he fell very quickly because he was not wearing his flying cape to glide safely to the ground. My goodness! He was in terrible danger.

Twinkly screamed, Scruffy hid, and everyone held their breath as poor Totalee fell down and down towards the ground. But, as I have said, Totalee was not like the other *Leaf Painters* and so he did not panic. Quite the opposite. As he fell, he simply thought, quite calmly, how he could avoid a rather bumpy and painful landing. As quick as a flash, he grabbed a leaf as he was falling and then did something quite remarkable. He stood on it. In fact, he surfed the leaf downwards through the air and then glided away from the ground and swooped back up into the air again. He flew past Twinkly, he triple-looped passed Scruffy (he would be dealt with later), and he soared above everyone high into the sky and whooped with excitement.

"WOO-HOO! I'M AIR SURFING.
CHECK THIS OUT!"

Everyone watched Totalee glide, twist, loop, and swoop. All the *Leaf Painters* were amazed. Eventually he landed safely, which took some considerable time because Totalee was having so much fun and had flown a very long way. But can you guess where he landed? Yes, that's right. Slap bang in the middle of Boring Snoring Land.

He was so excited that he had invented what would later become known as Leaf Surfing that he just wanted to invent some more games. In that same afternoon, which was not dull and boring at all now, he found the hills were good for Leaf Tobogganing...

... the streams were good for Leaf Canoeing...

... and the paths were excellent for Leaf Hurdling.

Totalee was having so much fun he had not realised that everyone, including a rather nervous-looking Scruffy, had been watching him from the edge of the trees. When he finally ran out of puff, which was just before buttercup teatime, he turned to make his way home and saw all the faces staring at him. He saw the Elders were at the front of the crowd. *Oh dear!* he thought, *I'm in the* deepest *of double trouble.* But then Scruffy started to clap, then Twinkly cheered, and then everyone shouted, including the Elders.

"HOORAY FOR TOTALEE TOMTUM!
HOORAY FOR THE MOST FANTASTICAL
OLYMPIC GAMES INVENTOR!"

Casperoon Eartheater called a special meeting that very evening. If the truth be known, and the Elders always told the truth, they had been looking for something to do once the leaves fell in deepest winter. So, from that time on, the *Leaf Painters'* Most Fantastical Olympic Games was to take place on the day the last leaf fell. Boring Snoring Land was renamed 'Totalee's Fantastical Land'. The newly invented games would continue until the first new (albeit dreary grey) leaf had grown.

The games became a huge success, and everyone loved them. All thanks to a little boy called Totalee, who was a little bit different, or perhaps I should say a little bit special.

But Totalee did not stop there. He went on to invent many other games: Leaf Frisbee, Leaf Skating, Volley Leaf... He is still inventing games to this very day. As for naughty Scruffy McQuinn, well, the Elders invented a new game just for him – tidying up all the leaves used in the games. They called it 'Turning over a New Leaf Game', but only Scruffy got to play it – every year. Serves him right, wouldn't you say?

Totalee never had to paint a single leaf again in his life. He had been excused by the Elders. In fact, they officially appointed him the Most Fantastical Olympic Games Inventor, which meant that he got to wear a special medal. Nobody ever understood why he did not like painting leaves, but it was obvious to everyone (including the trees) that he certainly loved playing with them.

Nearly the End

The next time you see a little boy or girl who is a little different, perhaps you should get to know them and see if they have a special talent. After all, they may be a games inventor like Totalee or something even more fantastical. Wouldn't that be fun?

Do you ever invent games? Well, if you ever do, Totalee would say, "That's totally fantastical! GAME ON! Come and find my Totalee Fantastical Land on our secret map. CATCH YOU LATER!"

Really the End... of this adventure.
Come join the Leaf Painters for the next one.

Half a Secret

Have you ever wondered why leaves are different shapes? Do you know who has something to do with it? Go on, guess! Yes – well, you are halfway right.

The *Leaf Painters* certainly are half responsible for Leaf Shaping, as it became known, but who was responsible for the other half? Well, I will tell you that shortly, but first you need to know what life, or rather leaves, were like before things changed.

Now, I want you to look at your fingernails. Imagine that your nails are now the colour of fresh green salad. And now picture your fingers as little twigs holding your little green nails. Wiggle them as if they are swaying in the wind. Do you know what you are looking at? Well, let me tell you. You are looking at the very first ever leaf shape. You see, the *Leaf Painters* know that new leaves are nail-shaped because they are the trees' nails, which is probably why the trees like to have them painted. So, your nails are at the end of your little fingers and the trees' leafy nails are at the end of their little twigs. Do you see?

Now where was I? Oh yes, I was telling you that someone else is half responsible for Leaf Shaping. Can you keep a secret? I hope so. Do you know, there are other small folk who live in the world of *Outside*? The *Leaf Painters* do. They used to call them the teeny-tiny small folk who happened to live in the fields, hills, rivers, rocks, and so on and so on. But because all the little folk in the world *Outside* were busy as bees doing busy things, they never really got to know each other and were happy to keep to themselves. But they knew that each other existed. In fact, the *Leaf Painters* were very well known to other teeny-tiny small folk. No, not as the *Leaf Painters*, but simply the little folk who happened to live in the woods and wore flying capes. But that was all about to change.

Once upon a very exciting afternoon, the *Leaf Painters'* Most Fantastical Olympic Games were well underway in Totalee's Fantastical Land. However, whilst everyone else played games, shouting, cheering, and enjoying themselves, Franacken Petalblower was bored. Yes, that is what I said. Absolutely, yawning bored.

You see, Franacken loves to paint, as you well know, and he really does not like to do anything else whatsoever ever. The Elders had been kind enough to let him paint the leaf medals for the Olympics in gold, silver, and bronze. But that was promptly dealt with in one short afternoon, and by the time he finished mixing his fresh green salad paint ready for the season known as spring, he was bored, bored, bored!

Franacken sat quietly at the edge of the woods sulking. How he desperately wished the first leaf would grow so the painting and real fun could begin. Poor Franacken.

But then the very exciting thing happened! It started when Franacken made a new friend after he heard the faintest of sounds. It was the sound of drumming fingers and it was coming from inside the hollow of an old log right by the edge of the snow-covered grass fields. He then heard a sigh, and then another sigh, and then some more drumming. Someone else was fed up, he thought, and almost certainly bored. So, he got up and crept quietly towards the log to investigate. He looked into the dark hollow and then heard a loud bark – "Woof! Woof!"

So, he ran back and hid behind a tree.

After a time, he peered at the log from his hiding place and then all of sudden a little man appeared, and when I say little, he was teeny-tiny small, even smaller than Franacken. Can you imagine? He came up to Franacken's knees, which for you means he was as tall as your thumbnail. The littlest of little folk, wouldn't you say? He had long, flowing curly green hair, a blue jacket, red shoes and he had a climbing rope with a hook at the end, which was tied around his waist. On his head he wore a round blue and green striped hat, and the hat seemed to move all by itself. A very interesting-looking little chap indeed.

The little man walked up boldly to Franacken and boomed: "Hello. I'm Vinni Van Bunzy, chief of the *Grass Shapers*, and this is Oakzy."

With that, the blue and green hat jumped off his head and barked. You see, it was not a hat, but an even teenier-tinier smaller barking beetle.

"Woof! Woof!" it barked again, which must have meant "Hello! Hello!"

Franacken was a bit scared of the beetle and fell backwards into a freshly made pot of his green salad paint. Poor Franacken. He was covered in his marmalade paint.

"Don't worry," said Vinni, "he won't bite. He only nibbles and trims the grass – he is a Barber Beetle."

By now the beetle was licking Franacken all over, which made the young artist giggle and wriggle A LOT. The pet beetle obviously liked the taste of the marmalade-flavoured paint. Vinni Van Bunzy put the teeny-tiny beetle back on his very teeny-tiny lead.

"A Barber Beetle?" exclaimed a now very wet and sticky Franacken. "I have never heard of such a thing, or, for that matter, of *Grass Shapers*. What do you do, friend, and more importantly, what are you doing in my woods?"

"Well, to tell the truth, and I always do, I'm double-yawny bored," said Vinni. "You see, there is not much for *Grass Shapers* to do at this time of year." Franacken completely understood how this felt.

"I heard the noise of the games and so decided to watch whilst I wait for the grass to start growing again," Vinni said. "You see, grass is lazy over the winter months and sleeps for a long time before it starts to grow properly." This was true. If you have sharp eyes, you may have noticed that the *Grass Shapers* start cutting their beloved grass long after the new leaves have started to bud and grow. Grass loves to sleep through winter, and spring has generally sprung before it really gets growing. The trees can often be heard whispering to the grass, "Wake up, you sleepy heads."

"You find it interesting when the grass grows? Why?" asked Franacken.

"Because then we can trim the grass." Vinni exclaimed. But Franacken was confused. Why would anyone want to trim grass? he thought.

Vinni could see he needed to explain himself a little more to this larger folk. Obviously being bigger does not always mean being smarter. "My dear friend, when grass eventually wakes up, it wakes up like an excited young child. It then grows upwards too quickly and too strongly as if to say to the world, *'Yippee, I'm awake, and I am tall, and I am strong, so watch me grow.'* So, you see, the new grass is very strong and stiff, like a bed of sharp prickly thorns. As the grass field is my home, we trim and soften the grass to sleep on. You wouldn't want to sleep on prickly grass, would you?"

"Er... I suppose not," said a rather bewildered Franacken, "but how do you trim grass? It is rather trim to start with in the first place after all."

With that, Oakzy the Barber Beetle jumped onto Vinni's head and barked and wiggled his beetle bottom like a dog would wag its tail.

"I've already introduced you. Our pet beetles do the trimming. Don't you, my good little Oakzy?" Vinni said, reaching up and tickling Oakzy's tummy.

More frantic barking and panting followed. "Woof! Woof Woofy Woof!" Barber Beetles do love having their tummies tickled.

Vinni suddenly blushed. "Do you think...?" he said. "Do you think the *Grass Shapers* can join in your games whilst we wait for the grass to grow? Your games look very exciting. Very exciting indeed."

"Of course you can," said Franacken without any hesitation. "I'm sure the Elders would agree. The more, the merrier, and us *Leaf Painters* simply love being merrier. But soon, I'm afraid, the games will end as the new leaves are almost here. What will you do whilst we start painting them? Leaves always arrive before the grass wakes up. You will be bored again."

Both of the little chaps sighed. It was a gloomy thought.

"No matter," said Vinni. "At least we have *something* to do for *some* of our quiet, boring time. Something is always better than nothing. Anyway," he said, changing the subject, "what are those?" Vinni pointed at the leaf medals.

"Oh, they are leaf medals that I painted for our Most Fantastical Olympic Games." Franacken handed Vinni a gold leaf medal.

"It is very well painted," said Vinni, which made Franacken blush, "but, hmmm, do you mind if I do something?" The artist nodded to show his approval and watched with interest as his new teeny-tiny little friend took out a piece of charcoal from his pocket and drew on the leaf. He drew one thick line down the middle and several fine lines from the edge of the leaf to the centre. He then drew all the way around the inside of the edge.

"I like to draw lines. I call the ones in the middle life lines," he said. "I draw lines on the grass for Oakzy to follow and trim to make the grass soft."

"Oh," said Franacken, who then thought *Oh no!* because as soon as Vinni had stopped drawing, Oakzy the Barber Beetle jumped off his master's head, barked and then, quick as a flash, trimmed Franacken's precious gold leaf medal.

"Woof! Woof!" barked the very excited beetle as it fetched the finished leaf and dropped it at the feet of the now very sad artist.

But, after a moment, Franacken looked at his precious leaf and could not help but smile. It had been improved, and goodness gumdrops, it was beautiful. Yes, yes, it really was fantastically beautiful indeed. Much more interesting than the same old nail shape.

"Well done, you two. Very well done!" cried Franacken.

Then suddenly, Franacken had an idea, a most wonderful idea. He blurted it out aloud to his new friend. "Vinni Van Bunzy, Oakzy and all of the *Grass Shapers* will *never* be bored again, I say, AND neither will I."

Vinni looked confused but tingled with excitement and anticipation at the same time. "From this day on," Franacken said, "whilst your lazy grass sleeps, you and your *Shapers* and clever Barber Beetles will draw and trim some designs on my stock of unused medal leaves to make new shapes. We will then choose the best designs to use for the new leaves. The *Grass Shapers* can draw those lovely life lines on the new leaves as they grow and then your clever beetles can trim them into the wonderful new shapes." Franacken did not stop for breath but continued excitedly. "Every tree should have a different-shaped leaf. As soon as a leaf is cut and trimmed, the *Leaf Painters* will then paint them. The trees will look more beautiful than ever. That will keep us ALL busy, and by the time we finish, your sleepy grass will have woken up. What do you think?"

Vinni was tingly-tangly thrilled but also a little nervous as he looked up at the tall trees and gulped. *Oh my goodness!* he thought. They were very tall, very neck-strainingly tall indeed. But then the trees, which had been listening to this conversation, started to sway with excitement and whispered, "Please do it, little Vinni Van Bunzy. We will keep you safe." Vinni took another gulp, Oakzy yapped and then they both nodded excitedly in agreement.

That very exciting afternoon ended with a big meeting of the Elders of both the *Leaf Painters* and the *Grass Shapers* in Totalee's Fantastical Land. Everyone listened as Franacken and his new teeny-tiny friend explained their plan. Casperoon Eartheater held up the newly shaped leaf in his hand and admired it. He then gave it to the eldest of the Elders of the *Grass Shapers*, Mossie Maple Wonzy. She also loved it and was extremely happy. So Casperoon exclaimed, "If the wise and honourable Elders of our new friends the *Grass Shapers* agree, then when the last leaf falls and your grass falls asleep, we welcome you all to play in our Most Fantastical Olympic Games. When you are not playing games, you may work with our Master Leaf Painter Franacken Petalblower to design beautiful new shapes for our beautiful trees. This will keep you busy before spring has finally sprung and before your sacred, though a little bit lazy, grass wakes up."

There was hush as Mossie turned to her Elders. The extremely teeny-tiny little folk huddled together and whispered. In truth, there had been some concerns about whether their ropes would be long enough to get everyone down safely from the mighty trees. Well, you can imagine how tall the trees would look to the *Grass Shapers*, can't you? But it was quickly decided that new longer rope could easily be made, of course. So that is exactly what the *Grass Shapers* would do. New longer rope. Simple!

Mossie proclaimed, "On behalf of my shapers and our pet Barber Beetles, we accept our new friends' offer of games, merriment, and exciting new work. From this day forward, we will never be gloomy and bored again." Everyone cheered and the Barber beetles woofed. "HOORAY FOR VINNI VAN BUNZY! HOORAY FOR THE *LEAF SHAPER!*"

And so, every year from that day on, new leaves had new shapes rather than just looking like your fingernails. The trees liked their leaves being trimmed. It tickled just like the brushes did, and after all, leaves are just tree nails so it did not hurt them. Franacken named every new shape leaf, and the trees that held them, after the *Grass Shapers'* pet Barber Beetles. The leaves that Oakzy trimmed became known as the leaves of the oak tree. Oakzy's friends Elmo, Birchy and Beechey had the trees elm, birch and beech named after them. The little beetles were all very proud of themselves.

Everyone was a little sad when the *Grass Shapers* left to trim the new grass when it eventually woke up, but they were happy to know that the winter would never be dull and double-boring again for anyone. Especially for Franacken, who now had all the new shapes to consider and select before spring sprang and he loved the new names for the trees.

By the way, all the trees were very pleased with their new names and newly shaped leaves. Before then, they were just known as, well, trees. And when you are tall and mighty like a tree, you really ought to have a proper name, shouldn't you?

Nearly the End

So the next time you visit the world of *Outside*, take a close look at the different trees and whisper their name. Place your hand on the trunk of the mighty oak and whisper very quietly, "I know why you are called an oak tree. It's because of your leaves." If the top branches sway, you will have made the oak tree very happy, and if you listen, you may hear the mighty oak tree whisper back to you, "Thanks for noticing, little one, but do keep our teeny-tiny little secret."

Really the End... of this adventure.
Come join the Leaf Painters for the next one.

What a MESS!

Do you remember the story of Franacken Petalblower and the first time he painted the leaves? Do you recall that everyone was worried because the leaves fell off in winter but cheered and celebrated when the new grey leaves grew back again in spring, ready to be shaped and painted? Well, there was one of the small folk in the world of *Outside* who did not cheer and applaud Franacken the *Leaf Painter*. He, in fact, did not like the young artist AT ALL. NOT ONE MEASLEY BIT! Why, I hear you say, was this little chap upset? Well, let us hear his story and you can decide. But before I tell it, it is only proper that you should meet this grumpy person, who at 1,680 years of age is considered very old even by *Leaf Painters* standards.

"GO AWAY! I AM GROUCHY GOBMAN AND I AM TOO BUSY TO TALK TO THE LIKES OF YOU!"

How rude! That isn't very polite, is it? Well, I shall have to tell his story instead as he is not very chatty, is he? And why is he wearing a hard hat made from a prickly horse chestnut seed AND where is his cape? All good questions and all will be revealed.

As I was saying before Grouchy's rude little outburst, there is a reason why Grouchy

does not like Franacken, or anyone else for that matter, but you may think differently of him when you learn a little more.

It is well known that all the *Leaf Painters* live way up high in their beloved trees in what they call their nestle nests. They look like a bird's nest from the ground but, if you look closely, they have a little chimney made from a reed that you can find growing near rivers and lakes. A very cosy little place, as long as you don't mind living very high up indeed.

But did you know there is only one *Leaf Painter* who is scared of heights? Can you guess who that is? It's Grouchy Gobman. He likes to live safely on the ground where the pine trees grow. That is why he has no need for a flying cape. He does not live in a nestle nest either, but in a discarded biscuit tin, which he found in a pile of rubbish. It does have a chimney though, which is made from a piece of garden hose. Grouchy is very good at recycling and making things, you see.

Grouchy truly loves his little house, which he considers to be far superior to the flimsy nestle nests. He also loves living under his sacred pine trees. Firstly, because *Leaf Painters*, who prefer to live up in oak or elm trees, do not bother him here. And secondly, the leaves of the pine tree are not constantly painted by the other *Leaf Painters*, so they never get heavy with paint and fall off and land on his head. Falling leaves hurt A LOT, which is why he wears his silly hard hat.

By the way, Franacken did paint the pine leaves – I should really say the pine *needles* – green once, but the paint kept dripping off. Pine needles are very fiddly to paint. So, they were left painted with one coat of fresh salad green all year round and their green leaves never got too heavy for the twigs to hold. Pine trees want to be painted different colours, you know, and are a little sad to be left out of all the fun. If you listen carefully, you can hear them whine and 'pine' to be painted, which is why they were first known as pining trees. Over time this was shortened to pine trees by Grouchy, who loves them just the way they are. So, there you have it, a lonely little chap living in a sad little wood all by himself. But this is how Grouchy Gobman liked it. Nice and quiet and no leaves dropping on his poor head.

Once upon a very annoying afternoon (it was only annoying for Grouchy, everyone was celebrating with Franacken that the new leaves had just grown) all the *Leaf Painters* were painting with fresh green salad paint and singing merrily. Grouchy, on the other hand, looked around at all the dead leaves on the woodland floor and sighed. You see, Grouchy Gobman was the official Keeper of the Woods and had been for the last 1,500 years, give or take a decade. He was without doubt the busiest of all the *Leaf Painters*, attending to his never-ending list of chores.

Grouchy's most important and favourite job was planting seeds and deciding where the new trees should grow. Well, you didn't think trees in the world of *Outside* grew just anywhere they liked, did you? No, every year Grouchy would collect the very best and strongest seeds and find a little space in the sunlight for them to grow. His other job, which he hated, was clearing up rubbish so that his precious little trees had enough space to grow freely. This job got more and more difficult every year. Not only did he have to deal with hard metal, plastics and smelly rubbish left by the giant folk (more about them later), but now he had all these chocolate-painted leaves to tidy away as well. The leaves never used to fall before Franacken Petalblower came along with his awful paint. AND it was much harder to find seeds under all those dead leaves. AND it did not help that his eyesight was getting worse in his old age (not that he would ever admit this or the fact that he was also slightly deaf). Poor Grouchy. Are you beginning to understand why he is so grumpy? Well, that is a lot of work to do on your own, isn't it?

Fortunately, Casperoon Eartheater, the eldest of the Elders and old school chum of Grouchy, could see his friend was even grumpier than usual. Nobody else noticed, by the way. There is not much difference between 'slightly' grumpy and 'extremely' grumpy, is there? But Casperoon knew his old friend well and he *could* tell the difference. Believe it or not, he was very fond of his silly old friend. He called down to the woodland floor where Grouchy was now shouting and waving his fist at Franacken, jumping up and down and kicking all the leaves. What a terrible fuss he was making.

"Grouchy, old boy!" called Casperoon. But Grouchy did not hear the Elder, and Casperoon, remembering his friend was a little deaf, glided down to the ground with his cape flapping behind him. He landed softly behind Grouchy, who was now rolling on the leaves and was throwing a terrible tantrum, which is a shameful way for an old man of 1,680 years of age to act, isn't it?

He repeated, a little more loudly, "Grouchy, old boy!"

Still nothing, so he yelled, "GROUCHY!"

This time his old friend jumped out of his skin, did a somersault, and landed hard on his bottom. Really hard!

"OOOOOOOH! My poor bottom!" he wailed and then continued to complain, "There's no need to shout, you old fool. I'm not deaf, you know. What do you want? I'm very busy thanks to your silly young artist Franacken Petalblower."

Casperoon, being very wise, had realised the problem the dead leaves would cause and so said calmly, "My dear old friend, I have come from a meeting with the Elders, and we have some good news for you."

"You have some good *chews* for me? I don't like sweets. They rot your teeth and I only have a few left."

"No, *NEWS*," Casperoon said a little louder. "What with all these leaves to clear, we have appointed a young apprentice to help you. After all, none of us are getting any younger."

This, Grouchy did hear. "You speak for yourself. I'm as fit as a young thousand year-old."

Ignoring his friend, which he often did, Casperoon continued and, looking up, he pointed to the sky and exclaimed, "And here she comes!"

Grouchy looked up in terror as a large bat swooped down towards him, knocked off his horse chestnut hat and scattered a pile of leaves that he had tidied earlier. What a mess!

"Good day to you, Sir. I am Tigerbella Firelight, and this is my bat Zakia."

"Tigerbella," snapped Casperoon, "come down off that beast and apologise to your new master for making a mess."

Tigerbella jumped out of her saddle. She strode over to Grouchy, handed him back his hat, slapped him on the back and grunted, "Sorry about that, old man. Still, you'll live, eh?"

Grouchy's face went pink, then red, then an angry purple. He turned to Casperoon and ranted, "I DON'T NEED AND WON'T HAVE AN APPRENTICE. NEVER EVER EVER! IF YOU STOP PAINTING THE

LEAVES SO THEY DON'T FALL OFF, THEN I'LL MANAGE JUST FINE THANK YOU! LEAVES SHOULD BE LEFT THEIR BEAUTIFUL GREY ANYWAY!" Grouchy was the only one of the *Leaf Painters* who actually liked the leaves in their original colour. He is a little odd, isn't he?

Casperoon shook his head and said firmly, "I'm sorry, old friend. It has already been decided by the Elders that Tigerbella will be your apprentice and help you clear the leaves for tree planting. She is young and stronger than any boy her age. Besides, some honest hard work will be good for her as she is a little excitable. IT IS FOR THE BEST!"

Grouchy's shoulders slumped. When an Elder said, "It is for the best," then ancient law said you must obey. After all, the Elders are, well, the eldest.

"Well, she better stay out of my way," he conceded.

Casperoon told Tigerbella not to pay any mind to the old fool, but it would be wise to keep her distance until they got to know each other.

For once, Tigerbella took the advice of her Elder and stayed out of Grouchy's way. In fact, she made a game of it. She liked hiding. She was very good at it, and it was, of course, pretty easy to hide from a little old chap who obviously had bad eyesight and was also a little deaf. But, as she watched Grouchy every day, something happened. She began to marvel at the way he chose his seeds with great care and fussed about where to plant them. He was very gentle when tending to his young sapling trees.

As the days turned to weeks, she could see that Grouchy was not at all grumpy as long as he was working with his sacred trees. He talked softly to the seeds as if they were his children and whispered to the young saplings. "Go on, my little friend, grow and be strong." And magically, the young trees did grow as soon as they were spoken to. It became obvious to Tigerbella that Grouchy was a magical wizard who simply loved his trees. But it was also obvious he was not keen on anything or anyone else. Silly but kind old wizard, she decided.

Tigerbella began to enjoy helping Grouchy because, like him, she too loved trees more than anything.

Very quietly she would hand him strong seeds she had found with her good sharp eyes. At first, he would throw them away and ignore her, but later at night, she saw him creep out of his biscuit tin house and pick up the discarded seeds and say "Sorry" before gently planting them. She would work very hard clearing leaves and rubbish left behind by the giant folk. She would fetch, carry, and hand Grouchy his trusty old spade for digging. She never spoke a word – she had quickly learnt that Grouchy was happiest when all was quiet and peaceful. The sounds of the woods and animals are truly magical if you take the time to listen to them, you know.

After months had passed, Grouchy would nod his head with approval when she did something right, but he would still growl at her if she did something ever so slightly wrong. He hardly ever spoke to her and he never ever smiled, but she did not mind. She was happy tending to the seeds and trees like her master did. She began to understand his anger for having to deal with all the rubbish they found every day. Clearing up the rubbish was a never-ending task.

One late and sad afternoon, Tigerbella found the old wizard kneeling and sobbing. She walked up to him and quietly placed her hand on his shoulder.

"Are you alright, Master Keeper?" Grouchy flinched at her touch.

"I'm fine. I'm fine. I just have something in my eye, that's all. Look! Someone has dumped oil all over one of my young trees."

Grouchy pointed to an old rusty can leaking oil all over the ground where a young sapling tree had been growing. The little tree was dying.

"Who would do such a horrible thing?" asked Tigerbella, who was now very angry and by instinct placed her hand on her trusty wooden sword.

"The giant folk from the City of Castles. We don't know *who* they are, so we call them *Who Mans*. Sometimes they come here in horseless carriages, which bellow out smelly black smoke. Then they dump

rubbish like this in my woods. They don't care for my trees." Grouchy sighed, "And so I clear up their mess, but it is getting harder every year."

Grouchy poured some water over the sick little tree and washed away the oil from its young leaves. He gently whispered a few words to it and stood up. "There," he said, "we can do no more. It is up to the tree now." The old man got up and walked slowly back to his home.

As Tigerbella watched the lonely figure disappear into the night, she felt sad. Why were these *Who Mans* so mean? Why didn't they love trees like she did? This must stop, she thought.

The next morning, Tigerbella and Grouchy went to see the young tree. To their huge relief, it had survived. For the first time since she had known him, Grouchy actually smiled. He even danced with joy with his young apprentice before he suddenly remembered that he hated dancing and stopped. He ordered Tigerbella to get on with her chores, which she did without any complaints or fuss. When she was not looking, he smiled again.

Over time, Tigerbella cleared all the leaves. She even got her bat Zakia to flap her wings to blow the leaves into neat piles so that Grouchy could plant his seeds.

They became a good team and worked very well together and, if truth be known, and Grouchy always told the truth, he had grown rather fond of his bat-flying apprentice. Grouchy even taught her a few magic words to whisper to the trees to help them grow. When Casperoon came to see how they were getting on, he was promptly told to go away by Grouchy AND Tigerbella. After all, they were BOTH very busy indeed.

Oh no, Casperoon shook his head and thought to himself. *Not another grumpy keeper to deal with!*

Right now, in the world *Outside*, the woods are kept very tidy thanks to Tigerbella and her master Grouchy. Zakia even lifts and clears all of the *Who Mans'* rubbish. As Tigerbella works, she hopes that most *Who Mans* are kind and that it is only a few naughty ones that leave rubbish behind. One day soon, my friends, she will get to meet the *Who Mans*, but that is another story and a very exciting one at that.

Nearly the End

Now you know what happens to the leaves that fall, and who plants seeds for the trees to grow, clears up all the rubbish, AND why an old wizard gets a little cross and grumpy from time to time. Wouldn't you?

What do you do with your rubbish when you go in the woods? I hope you always put it in a bin or take it home with you, because if you do, even Grouchy Gobman would smile at you and whisper from his hiding place, "Thank you very much, my young friend." But do not expect him to dance!

Really the End... of this adventure.
Come join the Leaf Painters for the next one.

BUBBLE! BANG! WHOOSH!

O ne day in the world of *Outside*, nearly everybody was cross. This was because nearly everybody was covered in paint, and many were covered in bruises too. And now all were gathered at the Naughty Step to see the culprit receive his punishment from the Elders.

Casperoon Eartheater approached the young boy and sighed heavily. So far, he had seen this boy on the Naughty Step 699 times, today made it a round 700. Yet another new *Outside* world record!

The boy, who was dressed in the shabbiest of clothes, smiled as the Elder approached because he was not frightened at all. He was *used* to getting into mischief. Can you guess who it was? Well, let's find out.

"Hello, Casperoon. I've done nothing wrong, you know, honest!" shouted Scruffy McQuinn.

Casperoon sighed again. This was the problem. Scruffy McQuinn never thought he *had* done anything wrong. Never ever! But today he had been extremely naughty. He had spent all morning painting twigs, branches, and yes, even his fellow *Leaf Painters*. And there he stood. Smiling proudly at anyone who cared to look at him.

"It was only a bit of fun, old man," Scruffy continued. "You should have seen everyone slipping on my paint. What a laugh! I love paint. Isn't it great to be a *Leaf Painter*? Woooo hooooh!"

Casperoon, for once, was speechless. After 699 punishments, he still could not change the boy. He put his head in his hands and thought a terrible thought. For the first time ever, he would have to banish one of his own kind from the woods. He was very sad that it had come to this.

"Casperoon, I have an idea," someone shouted from the back of the crowd. Everyone turned to see who it was. Franacken Petalblower stepped forward and approached the Naughty Step.

As far as Casperoon was concerned, this day was turning out to be a very strange one indeed. First, he had a boy who would never learn to behave, and NOW he had a non-Elder interfering with Elders' business – most irregular. He gave up, sat down, and huffed. He decided to let Franacken speak. *What harm could it do?* he thought.

Scruffy was very amused by all the excitement. Franacken joined the young boy on the step, put his hand on the culprit's shoulder and smiled. There were audible gasps in the crowd. Franacken waited for everyone to settle down, and when they did, he spoke softly.

"Many of you will all remember that I, Franacken Petalblower, once stood on this step for similar crimes. I too painted some of you and most of your pets, for that matter." There were a few angry-looking folk nodding in agreement. "But," Franacken continued, "I learnt to become helpful rather than hurtful. I think Scruffy can change his naughty ways too."

Everyone had long since forgiven Franacken for his past crimes, but to expect Scruffy to suddenly become helpful was a ridiculous idea. There were jeers, boos, and cries of "Shame!" It was clear they thought Franacken was nothing like Scruffy. After all, Franacken had only been on the Naughty Step several times, not several hundred times. The general consensus was that Scruffy McQuinn was a bad, smelly, icky egg and he simply had to GO!

Franacken waited patiently until the noise died down. He turned to Scruffy, who by now was thrilled with all the attention he was receiving and was grinning from ear to ear. "Scruffy," began Franacken, "do you like my paint?"

"NO!" Scruffy giggled. "I don't *like* your paint, Franacken, I LOVE your paint. I love the way it makes things like branches slippery, the way it sticks to my fingers and everyone's clothes, AND I REALLY LOVE the smell of it. Mmmm... sweet marmalade. I'LL SAY IT AGAIN. ISN'T IT GREAT TO BE A *LEAF PAINTER*! SKIPPERTY DIPPERTY!"

The young boy was by now rolling about at Franacken's feet having a *huge* giggling fit. It was a shameful display by a *shameless* boy. And if that was not enough, Scruffy began to sing a silly song and giggle at the same time.

BUBBLE! BANG! WHOOSH!

Scruffy's Song

One two three four five
Once I painted a fish alive
And when I was done with that
I painted my mummy and my cat

The Elders say that I am bad
But you know that they're just sad
So I paint their trousers gold
That way they don't look so old

But the thing that busts my sides
Is sloppy paint that makes folk slide
Oh, it is so much fun
To see you all land on your...

"ENOUGH!" boomed Casperoon before Scruffy could finish... thank goodness.

Everybody, including Scruffy McQuinn, became very quiet. Casperoon continued, "Franacken! Give me one good reason why I should not pass the biggest of the biggest scary punishments for young McQuinn."

Then there was a sudden outburst from the crowd as Scruffy's mother, NooNoo McQuinn, barged her way forward to the front of the crowd and fell at Casperoon's feet sobbing loudly.

"Please, Casperoon Eartheater. Please don't banish my son."

Casperoon was touched by her plea, but what choice did he have? Enough was surely enough. But then Franacken exclaimed, "Casperoon, the boy could work for me from now on and I will see to it that he behaves." He stepped forward, smiled and helped NooNoo to her feet. He spoke confidently, "Scruffy McQuinn will do no harm to any of you from this day forth because from today he will be doing his favourite thing. He will help me make my paint."

"Yippity Skipperty Dipperty!" whooped Scruffy. He then did three cartwheels, two somersaults, and five roly-polies. He was so excited and dizzy he did not hear Casperoon give his blessing to Franacken's idea.

"BUT," Casperoon bellowed, "if Scruffy McQuinn causes any more upset, then he will be banished FOREVER TIMES A HUNDRED!"

NooNoo was mightily relieved. Franacken was happy, and Scruffy kissed everyone and everything, including Grouchy Gobman.

The very next morning, Scruffy arrived bright and early under the Elders' Most Sacred and Holy

Ancient Tree, which is where Franacken made his paint at his paint factory. Scruffy was very excited. He waited outside a huge tipi made from twigs and leaves that bore the sign 'Franacken's Paint Works – DO NOT ENTER!' Suddenly, two large leaf doors parted and out stepped his new master covered in freshly made summer blossom paint. Even Scruffy admired Franacken, and for once he was a little more serious rather than silly.

"Good morning, Franacken Petalblower, Sir... I mean Master Petalblower. I'm very excited to be here, Sir... er, Master, I mean. My mum says I will be in serious double trouble if I don't behave, but I really want to because I really, really, really..."

"Love paint?" Franacken smiled. "Yes, I know. Well, come with me into my factory." Franacken went back through the leaf double doors, closely followed by his young and very excitable apprentice. As soon as Scruffy stepped through the doors, he froze and stared at the magnificent scene before him. The inside of the tipi was huge. He looked up and up and up, but he could not see where the top ended. Then he looked across. It seemed the other side of the tepee was wider than the whole forest. It had to be some kind of magic.

On the ground were hundreds, no thousands, of cauldrons, all with fires beneath them. Steam rose from them and created a cloud high at the very top of the tipi and absolutely everything smelt of scrummy marmalade.

All Scruffy could keep saying was "Yipperty Dipperty."

"I know," said Franacken. "It's pretty fantastical, isn't it? Anyway, now to work. Follow me."

Franacken spent the next few weeks showing his young apprentice how to mix different coloured flowers with water and, yes, marmalade to make hundreds of different coloured paints. He showed him how to warm the paint so it became sticky and then boil the paint so it would become shiny. Franacken explained many times that warming was done with the cauldron lid on and boiling was done with the lid off. Never the other way around. Every day he said, "You must never ever boil the paint with the lid on. Never! It is extremely dangerous."

Once at the end of a very long afternoon, Franacken said Scruffy could make some paint of his own. Scruffy was delighted and so excited that he wanted to start immediately. "No," Franacken snapped. "It's getting dark and the *Who Mans* have their Firework Night tonight. I am sure you would like to join everyone and watch it... from a very safe distance, of course. You can mix your own paint tomorrow. Now sweep up and tidy. And Scruffy, remember to take the lids off the cauldrons before you leave as the paints are starting to boil."

Scruffy, who was now quite an obedient apprentice, picked up his broom and started to sweep. He watched Franacken leave and finished tidying very quickly because he could not wait to rush off to tell his mother that tomorrow he would be allowed to make his very own paint. "Whoopee!"

That night, everyone had gathered in a clearing at the edge of the forest. They were looking up into the sky. In the distance, where the *Who Mans* lived in their City of Castles, the night sky was alive with bright colours, sights, and sounds. Fireworks Night!

Scruffy loved the colours that lit up the night sky, but he was frightened by the loud bangs and whooshing sounds. He was getting more and more scared as the noise got louder and louder. In fact, these were the loudest fireworks he had ever heard. The sounds were deafening, but then he suddenly realised the noises were coming from behind him and not from the *Who Mans'* fireworks at all. He turned around, and his eyes widened in horror. "Oh no, I forgot to take the lids off the cauldrons!"

Scruffy opened the factory doors and peered inside. The paint was not boiling; it was exploding! In fact, there were multi-coloured fountains and jets of paint erupting from all the cauldrons. The lids of cauldrons rocketed into the air. BUBBLE! BANG! WHOOSH! Different coloured paints shot up higher and higher, ripping the top of the tipi and spurting out into the night sky. Up and up and up the paint exploded.

"Oh no, what am I going to do?" Scruffy panicked and did what he always did in moments like this. He ran and hid in a *Who Man's* discarded smelly old sock!

The crowd that had gathered to watch the *Who Mans'* firework display had now turned around to watch an exploding, well, *paintwork display.* Beautiful and exciting colours shot up into the air from Franacken's tipi, high up into the branches of the Elders' Most Sacred and Ancient Tree. The tree was soaked with a multitude of different coloured paints. The lids from the cauldrons whizzed and spun through the air like Frisbees and made whistling noises, whilst the exploding paint made bangs and whooshing sounds.

Bubble! Weeee! Ziiiipppp! Bang! Whoosh!

Everybody cheered as the paint covered the twigs and leaves at the very top of the sacred tree.

The next morning, a very frightened Scruffy eventually came out of his hiding place. But then, to his amazement, he heard cheering from a crowd standing underneath the Elders' Most Sacred and Ancient Tree. He looked up at the tree and gazed in wonder at its leaves. There were reds, golds, yellows, greens, purples and browns.

"Scruffy McQuinn, come here!" screamed Franacken. "What have you done? Look at this mess! You must have left the lids on last night!"

Scruffy was about to apologise to his master when, to his surprise, Casperoon spoke up for him. "Don't be too hard on the boy, Franacken. Look how beautiful our sacred tree is. It is truly special now thanks to Scruffy's, for once, happy accident. Look!"

And Franacken did look at all the colours and had to agree. Never before had he seen such beautiful leaves. Suddenly everyone started to clap and chant, "Hooray for Scruffy, the King of Celebrations."

Scruffy had never been praised like this before – not ever. And do you know what? He rather liked it. A Skipperty Dipperty lot!

Soon the Elders decided that on one special night every year, Scruffy would be allowed to bubble up his paint with the lids kept on, letting all the paint explode. It became a major celebration, and it was called Scruffy's Paintworks Night. Good old Scruffy.

Nearly the End

The special night in question is November 5th, which happens to be the very same day many of us celebrate Guy Fawkes Night with bonfires and fireworks. So, you are unlikely to notice Paintworks Night, as you will be too busy enjoying Fireworks Night. But do take a look at the trees the next morning. Who knows? You may see a multi-coloured one. Go on, give it a try. If you do, you'll have Scruffy McQuinn to thank. But make sure the paint is dry before you touch it.

Really the End... of this adventure.
Do join the Leaf Painters for the next one.

Totalee's Discovery

The Games Inventor, Totalee Tomtum, was about to make a new discovery, but not the one he had been planning. The new discovery he had been planning to make was his new White-Water Leaf Canoeing course for this year's upcoming Olympics. He was sitting in his best canoe leaf ready to start the white-water ride. What a thrill! he thought.

He imagined a scene where everyone, including the animals of the woods, had come to cheer on the fearless Totalee Tomtum. He gave his own commentary, "Could the winner of no less than 126 Olympic gold leaf medals win yet another gold at his latest favourite sport?"

He continued talking to himself. "Amazing scenes here! Excitement erupts as the crowd spots their totally cool hero and greatest Fantastical Olympian of all time." Totalee Tomtum waved to his imaginary fans and then climbed into his speedy leaf canoe named Lightning Waves. All the other competitors who had attempted this dangerous new course had crashed and almost drowned in these wild waters of Blizzard Blossom Brook. His mother had begged him not to race, but Totalee laughs in the face of danger – HA HE HA HE HA – and was now only seconds away from his potential 127th gold leaf medal or, perhaps... certain death.

He has a very silly imagination, doesn't he? Especially as the waters of Blizzard Blossom Brook are more gentle than wild. In fact, Totalee added the name 'Blizzard' to what was once known as just Blossom Brook. Let's not spoil his fun though, and instead listen a little more to his excitable nonsense.

"As the crowd holds their breath, the young Olympian launches his leaf canoe with the unbelievable strength of a hamster. He disappears out of sight into the mist and torrents of the waters of rage."

If you were watching but not able to hear Totalee's exaggerations, he would look like a little chap sitting on a little leaf having a lovely gentle ride drifting along at about one millipede per hour. But do not be too harsh on him, because if you were only the size of half of your thumb, the gentle spring waters might look a little more dangerous.

"FANTASTICAL! I'm a white-water legend. Hooray for me!"

To be fair to Totalee, he did navigate his way around his new water course quite quickly. He cleared the Bay of Shipwrecks, which was in fact a small twig stuck in the mud. Then he dashed past the Rapids of Doom, which were more of a ripple. He was now fast approaching the Gorge of Chaos. But THAT was when the real discovery happened. Instead of entering the Gorge of Chaos, he suddenly crash-landed head-first into a giant metal wall. "OUCH! REALLY, REALLY OUCHY!" cried Totalee as he sat rubbing his poor head whilst looking up at the… big… shiny… metal thing?

He stumbled backwards whilst looking up, higher and higher, until he could finally make out what it was that had been dropped right in the middle of Blizzard Blossom Brook. It was a gigantic shovel.

"*WHO MANS!*" he screamed. Quickly, he ran back into the woods, only to bump into a rather angry-looking Grouchy Gobman. The panicky Totalee Tomtum knocked Grouchy to the ground and Grouchy's chestnut hard hat was sent flying.

Totalee could tell that the Keeper of the Woods was cross. He quickly scrambled to his feet and handed the old wizard his horse chestnut hat, but Grouchy was not looking at Totalee, and he did not seem to care about his hat. No, Grouchy was looking back at the shovel and then he looked up at the sky. He suddenly shouted, "Get out of the way, young Tomtum!"

Whilst Totalee was thinking, Get out of the way of what? a huge flying bat knocked him off his feet. When he looked up, he saw a pretty but serious looking young girl sitting astride the bat. It was Tigerbella Firelight and she looked angry too. She dismounted, tied her bat Zakia to a nearby tree and stroked him gently to calm him down. Zakia breathed heavily and was clearly tired. She fired a look at Totalee, which made him step backwards nervously. She then turned to her master.

"It is as you feared, Master Keeper. Another 100 of our trees have been lost this sad day. That makes over 300 lost so far and there are no signs of the *Who Mans* stopping. They are cutting down the mightiest and the eldest of our beloved trees. Then they load them onto giant horseless carriages, which take them away." Overcome with sadness, she sobbed. "What use are dead trees to them? There is no beauty in a lifeless tree."

Grouchy comforted her. "You have done well, Tigerbella. Now we must give our report to the Elders."

Later that day, Casperoon Eartheater called an emergency meeting of the Elders to listen to the reports given by Tigerbella and

Grouchy. Everyone gasped as they heard about the destruction of their trees and that the *Who Mans* were now moving even closer to their forest. Something had to be done.

Brave Tigerbella Firelight wanted to go into battle right there and rid the woods of the horrible and badly behaved *Who Mans*. But Casperoon said it would be folly to try and fight the giant folk. As the eldest of the Elders, he suggested that he should instead find the wisest of the *Who Mans* and hope the matter would be resolved quickly and peacefully. Never before had a meeting of the Elders been so lively. One half wanted to call all the *Leaf Painters* and the woodland animals to war, whilst the other half sided with Casperoon. The meeting went on late into the night and there was still no sign of anyone agreeing. But then Casperoon shuddered as he heard a familiar voice. His wife, who was also a very powerful witch, as you well know, approached.

"You're all excitable fools! The silliest of silly Billies!" shouted Winceyfloss Eartheater.

There was a hush as the old witch hobbled her way into the middle of the gathering. You may recall that witches always interfered in meetings of the Elders when there were difficult decisions to be made. Casperoon stepped to one side to let his wife speak. After all, he did not want to be turned into a snail, which was her latest favourite thing to do. She looked around at all the faces fiercely. There was complete silence.

"Casperoon is right." Her husband blushed with pride and was about to say, "Of course I am, my dear," when Winceyfloss exclaimed, "But he is also a little wrong!" Casperoon kept on blushing, but this time out of embarrassment. He stepped further away from his wife, who now seemed to be talking utter gobbledygook. "You see, we need to think fast, but we will have two tactics, not one," she explained. She looked at Tigerbella. "Young Keeper of the Woods, you shall have your battle, but you are NOT to risk lives. Instead, you must simply *slow* the *Who Mans* down a bit. My dear brave girl, my husband is right; the giant *Who Mans* cannot be beaten in battle. But whilst you keep them busy, Casperoon will seek out the wisest *Who Man* and agree for the tree destruction to stop."

So, there it was. Winceyfloss had spoken, and the two-tactic plan was agreed. Not that Winceyfloss asked for approval. But nobody was about to argue with a bossy witch, were they?

After the meeting had finished, Tigerbella saw Casperoon and her master Grouchy talking to something that looked like fireflies dancing and sparkling in the air. She hid and waited. Eventually, the lights flew away into the night and the two old friends parted company. However, Grouchy had seen her hiding and he was not happy. She should have been heading home to bed by now, but these days he found it very difficult to get cross with Tigerbella because, if truth be known, she reminded him of what he was like when he was a young, brave man.

"What were those dancing lights, Master Keeper? They looked like fireflies."

"You are too nosy for your own good, young lady, and you should be asleep," Grouchy snapped. Then his face softened as he realised that years ago, he would have asked the same question. So, he explained, "They are *Tree Spirits*, as ancient as the trees themselves. They, like us, protect the trees and help them grow. But they are very angry, and very sad. When a tree is felled by the *Who Mans*, one of their kind also dies with the tree."

This made Tigerbella even sadder. She began to weep. Even the nearby ants were too sad to put their umbrellas up and cried with Tigerbella. Trees and their sacred spirits were dying. Grouchy gave her a gentle hug. As she sobbed, she saw one of the little lights had returned and was coming straight towards her. As it hovered very close to her nose, Tigerbella could see it was a beautiful tiny woman with long golden hair and the tiniest blue lace wings that fluttered like the wings of a hummingbird. She glowed with a brilliant white light. Her striking blue eyes looked kindly at Tigerbella. Then she spoke, or at least Tigerbella thought she spoke, but the pretty mouth of the *Tree Spirit* did not move. Tigerbella was hearing the beautiful creature's thoughts. It was mind magic. "Young, brave Tigerbella, do not cry. The trees are fond of you and do not like to see your tears."

Tigerbella felt a little better for being comforted by the *Tree Spirit*. The magical spirit continued, "I am Princess Fernella. Tonight, the *Tree Spirits* and your wizards will summon a mighty army of woodland animals. So, you must rest now, my little one, and keep strong. Tomorrow you will be victorious, and all will be as it should."

The little figure then blew some sparkling dream dust towards Tigerbella's face. "Sleep, little one, and dream only good things." Tigerbella suddenly felt very drowsy. Grouchy felt the young girl go limp in his arms as she fell into a peaceful sleep. He gently laid her down on some soft moss. After he had tended to her, he turned to Princess Fernella, who now spoke to his mind using her magic.

"It has been done, old friend. I have summoned the warrior animals. The fearless red squirrels, the ferocious badgers, and the wild boar are on their way. You and your old friend must call the mighty fighting bats and the *Slow Ones*." She paused and looked over Grouchy's shoulder. "I see your fellow wizard approaches."

Grouchy bowed to the flying spirit. "We will do this tonight, my princess."

As Princess Fernella flew away, Grouchy turned to face the other wizard, who now stood by his side. It was Casperoon Eartheater. The two old magicians turned to face the darkest part of the forest, cupped their hands over their mouths. They appeared to call, but no sound came from their lips. Well, no sound that you or I could hear. However, the fighting bats certainly heard the secret call of their masters and began to fly to them. From deep beneath the ground, the *Slow Ones* also heard their call. Then they began to move through the earth with steely purpose. Tomorrow would be a very long day indeed.

Nearly the End

So, my friends, will Tigerbella be victorious in battle? Will Casperoon find a kind and good *Who Man?* AND just who are the *Slow Ones*? Well, all will be revealed tomorrow in the world of *Outside*.

Really the End... well, not quite.

Do join the Leaf Painters as the biggest adventure is coming.

The Slow Ones

Casperoon Eartheater and Grouchy Gobman stood on the lowest and thickest branch of the Elders' Most Sacred, and now multi-coloured, Ancient Tree. With hands on waists, they surveyed the scene below them. There was hardly any ground visible as an army of warrior animals joined the vast army of *Leaf Painters*. The fearless Red Squirrel Cavalry were carrying their brave *Leaf Painter* riders. The mighty badgers pulled heavy wooden carts filled with sticky stink bomb berries. The wild boar snorted and tugged excitably against their reigns, which were held by the riders perched upon their heads.

The army was almost complete... but not quite. One group had not arrived. But then Casperoon Eartheater looked down at the ground and shouted to the crowd below him, "STAND WELL BACK. HERE THEY COME!!"

Suddenly, the ground shook. *Leaf Painters* and animals ran out of the way and then turned to watch as the soil everywhere grew into huge mounds. Something was about to come out of the ground. The *Slow Ones* had arrived.

Totalee Tomtum had heard stories about these legendary warriors and was actually a little nervous. He hid behind his Leaf Surfboard and waited with everyone else to watch these magnificent creatures erupt from their world called *Underside*. And my goodness, erupt they did. Thousands of them appeared. Thousands and thousands of... earthworms!

Totalee could **not** believe it. All this fuss over some earthworms. Okay, they were wearing warrior helmets, but COME ON, LEGENDARY WARRIORS? Totalee started to giggle, and then he laughed. He rolled about shamelessly in absolute hysterics. He pointed at the warrior worms and just about managed to speak. "Oh, hail the mighty *Slow Ones*, the legendary..." he started to giggle again, "the legendary..." now he was laughing again, "WIGGLY WORMS!" He could not help himself and once again was rolling about on the floor in fits of giggles. "TEE HEE TIDDLY HEE, I can't believe I was nervous."

"Who said that?" snapped one of the worms (I mean to say, *warrior* earthworms). "Come down here. I'll suck your toe clean off."

The worm sounded scary enough to stop the naughty young Totalee from laughing. The angry earthworm continued. "Somebody throw me at 'im. I'll teach 'im to laugh at the mighty *Slow Ones*. I'll lasso 'im in knots. You're lucky, my friend, the centipedes are not here. They'd climb up there and kick you in the shin a hundred times, one kick by each foot!"

Now Totalee was truly nervous. The warrior earthworm raised out of the ground to try and find Totalee. He was huge and so long. The earthworm almost reached the lower branches of the tree Totalee was hiding in. Gigantic! He wished he had not been so disrespectful. Luckily for him, the angry warrior had poor eyesight. Totalee remained in his hiding place and decided, sensibly, to stay very quiet.

The warrior eventually calmed down. Clearly the young upstart had been silenced. "Good," he growled. "Whoever you are, young *Leaf Painter*, you would do well to remember that us *Slow Ones* may be the last to arrive to the battle, but we are always the very *last* to leave." He then shouted in the direction of Totalee, who was now shaking in his yellow boots with fear, "AND WE HAVE NEVER LOST A BATTLE YET – NEVER EVER EVER!!" Everyone cheered.

Totalee whispered, "Sorry, mighty warriors."

"ENOUGH!" boomed Casperoon Eartheater. "Knights of the *Slow Ones*, approach." Three of the largest and longest worms moved forward. They each wore silver warrior helmets and looked very important and fearless. They bowed in front of Casperoon. Casperoon's expression softened. "Welcome, Sir Slobalot, Sir Slimealot and Sir Snotalot." Totalee had to bite down on his own hand to stop himself from laughing again. "Have the preparations been made?" Casperoon asked.

"They have, Master Eartheater. We have worked through the night and built our largest stinky Goo-Trap yet. Our cousins from the swamps have stayed behind to join the fight too." *This is excellent news*, Casperoon thought. Last night he had ordered the warriors to go to the *Who Mans'* camp and surround their work shed with a huge Goo-Trap. This meant that the *Who Mans* could now not reach their horrible tools of destruction.

What is a Goo-Trap, you ask? Well, have you ever been stuck in really sticky mud? Mud so sticky that it can pull your boots off and socks too? Well, that special muddy bog is made sticky by the *Slow Ones*, and Sir Snotalot was particularly good at making it exceptionally sticky, as you can probably imagine.

Casperoon was very pleased. "Good work, my brave *Slow Ones*. Now I must ask you to set another Goo-Trap to protect our home should we need to retreat." The warriors nodded and the three knights, followed by their army of thousands, dived back down into the dark earth to the world of *Underside*. They vanished as quickly as they had appeared.

Casperoon looked over at his wife, Winceyfloss. She was sprinkling her most irritating itching powder over the sticky stink bomb berries piled up in the wooden carts pulled by the badgers. Yes, Casperoon was very pleased indeed with the preparations. But now he would have to leave them to go on his own mission to find a wise and most important *Who Man*. He turned to his old friend Grouchy and the muscle-bound leader of the Red Squirrel Cavalry. "Grouchy and Scottlee 'Bulldog' Bashem, I must leave you now. You know the plan. Good luck, my brave friends."

Bulldog handed the reigns of his red squirrel, Glidestar, to the Elder. "Take Glidestar, Casperoon. Glidestar is the fastest of all the red squirrels and the bravest. He will keep you safe." Casperoon thanked the warrior and mounted Glidestar, standing between the red squirrel's fluffy ears. Within seconds they had bounded into the forest and disappeared from sight.

And so it was left for Grouchy to lead the battle charge of the *Leaf Painters* and friends. He looked around at the army and for once he smiled. He then laughed wildly. This gave everyone courage as they had never seen Grouchy smile before, let alone laugh. Time to deal with those naughtiest of *Who Mans* at last. He then shouted skywards, "Tigerbella!"

Everyone looked up at the magnificent sight of Tigerbella Firelight riding her bat Zakia with great skill. The pair of them swooped down and landed softly by Grouchy's feet. "Yes, Master Keeper?"

"Well, my dear, it is time you learnt who you really are." Tigerbella was confused. What did Grouchy mean? The old master continued. "Casperoon Eartheater is the King of the *Slow Ones. I* am the King of the Battle Bats and *you*, my little one, have magic too. Casperoon did not make you my apprentice by accident, you know. You have a gift." Grouchy could see Tigerbella begin to mouth words, but she did not speak them, as if she were too afraid to say them out aloud. Then very quietly, she whispered almost to herself, "The insects, I've always believed I could hear their thoughts."

Grouchy laughed. "Yes, that's it, my dear girl. You are the Queen of the Insect Army. You can call the insects in the same way that I am able to call the loyal bats that now wait for my command. You must now summon the greatest and most feared of all the insect armies. Call the Harpoon Hornets!" He looked at Tigerbella and placed his hand on her shoulder to reassure her. "You can do it, Tigerbella. You always could."

Tigerbella took a deep breath. Then she cupped her hands over her mouth and made a call that nobody could hear. That is, of course, unless you were a hornet. And hundreds, no millions, did hear her call from miles and miles away. They now flew swiftly towards their queen. They knew it was time to go to war.

Nearly the End

Meanwhile, Glidestar bounded, climbed, swung, and galloped so quickly that Casperoon had to hold on to the squirrel's furry ears with all of his might. Soon he would be in the *Who Mans'* world of *Inside*, the vast City of Castles. He made a silent prayer that he would be successful in his quest and his friends would survive the battle ahead.

Really the End...
**well, not for this continuing and biggest adventure.
Do join the Leaf Painters to see what happens next!**

WHO MANS!

If the truth be known, and like the *Leaf Painters*, I always tell the truth, Mr. Williams is not a pleasant man at all. In fact, he is downright horrible and mean. Even the men that work for him do not like him – not one bit. He makes Grouchy Gobman look like an angel, even when Grouchy is in the worst of moods. Mr. Williams is as tall as he is round and looks like a beach ball with tiny legs, balding red hair, bad teeth, and icky stinky stale breath.

But Mr. Williams does not care one tiny bit about what others think of him. He is very happy because he is very rich and money is his *only* friend. He loves nothing more than to count his precious money. He makes all his money by breaking rules and being very sneaky. AND, as I am sure you have guessed, Mr. Williams is the *Who Man* who had started all the trouble. He is without doubt the naughtiest kind of *Who Man.*

You see, Mr. Williams had not been given permission to cut down the trees in the world of *Outside*, or anywhere else, for that matter. In fact, he had been completely banned from cutting down *any* beautiful trees. He never follows the rules, like you must plant new trees to replace the ones taken to make furniture. And so, he had absolutely no right to be in the sacred forest cutting down trees. But he did not care at all. And nobody realised what he was up to because the forest was far, far away from the world of *Inside*. Yes, he could be very sneaky as long as he was making a lot of his precious money. He rather loved the fact that he got away with complete and utter destruction. Isn't he awful?

Once on a very eventful morning, Mr. Williams made his way to his tree-cutting camp as usual. The camp itself was hidden by plastic bushes to hide his cutting machines. He opened the secret gates to his camp and made his way to the work shed, which he did every day. But this time he could not reach the work shed because a stinky, gooey, muddy bog completely surrounded it. How odd it must have looked. After all, it had not rained for days.

He hated mud as it always messed up his expensive designer clothes, which he had bought from his favourite shop, Orribly Rich Fashion. And so, he decided he would wait in his expensive car until his woodcutters arrived. "They can get messy instead of me!" he sneered.

After a struggle, he squeezed into his car seat. It was a very tight squeeze and his large, round tummy kept beeping the car horn. Finally seated, he read his favourite book, *Sneaky Business Tips for the Orribly Rich*.

From their hiding place in the woods, the *Leaf Painters* and their army of woodland friends watched and waited in silence. Grouchy Gobman stood on the head of the largest wild boar called Willoughby. He touched Willoughby's sharp armour-plated tusks that had been made for all of the Wild Boar Army. Everyone was in position, ready to attack. He saw Tigerbella Firelight and her faithful bat Zakia circling overhead, surrounded by hundreds and hundreds of bats and millions of Harpoon Hornets. He saw the mighty Scottlee 'Bulldog' Bashem sitting proudly ahead of his Red Squirrel Cavalry. Winceyfloss, the good but bossy old witch, spoke quietly to the badgers that pulled the wooden carts laden with her itchy, sticky stink bomb berries. She was pleased that the naughtiest *Who Man* had not reached the work shed and had now clearly fallen asleep in his strange horseless carriage. Everything was ready...

Far away from the forest, Casperoon was quite saddle sore and tired, but he was very relieved. He had at last found the wise *Who Man* he had been looking for. He dismounted Glidestar and walked into a pretty cottage garden where an old man was sitting fast asleep under a maple tree. Unbeknown to the other *Leaf Painters*, Casperoon had met the *Who Man* before and he knew this dear friend simply as 'Peter', for that was the good *Who Man's* name. He was a little surprised how Peter had aged in such a short time. After all, it was only 70 years or so since they had last met. But then he remembered how surprised Peter had been when they first met to learn that

Casperoon was 1,710 years old. Yes, he remembered, *Who Mans* are all youngsters really and sometimes act up like *all* children do. Peter

was not naughty, however. Peter was truly good.

Peter snored loudly under his favourite tree, dreaming of the time when he was a little boy and the adventures he had with wise old

Casperoon Eartheater. He had never told anyone about the *Leaf Painters* because he feared nobody would believe him. Worse still, it could have ruined the *Leaf Painters'* way of life if they had believed him.

Now he dreamed a very happy dream of the time he was told the secrets of the colour and shapes of the leaves. He dreamt that Casperoon had come back to see him again after all this time and was saying "Wake up, young man, wake up this instant!"

But, of course, he was *not* dreaming, was he? Casperoon *was* there and shouting very loudly indeed! The Elder was now in fact perched upon the sleeping giant's shoulder and was tickling Peter's nose with a feather, booming, "WAKE UP, YOUNG PETER. WAKE UP FOR GOODNESS' SAKE!"

Suddenly, Peter bolted upright and knocked poor Casperoon flying through the air across the entire garden. He landed in the birdbath and was completely soaked from cape to boot. Peter was about to say sorry, but Casperoon waved his arm to dismiss the matter because he had urgent business to attend to with *young* Peter the Good. Casperoon was still very sprightly for 1,780 and was able to jump onto the giant's shoulder in one big leap.

Standing by Peter's enormous *Who Man* ear, Casperoon began to tell his friend the sad tale of the mean tree cutters led by the despicable Mr. Williams. By the time he had finished, Peter was furious. But he was not sure if he could help. After all, who would believe that there were tiny folk who wore even tinier flying capes? Would you? He was very sad for his dear friend, but explained he had no obvious solution.

Casperoon felt helpless. He has been so sure Peter could save the day. The old wizard wept in desperation. As he sobbed, Glidestar approached, concerned for the wizard. Peter looked very closely at the squirrel and then smiled, and then he laughed and kept laughing with absolute joy!

"That's it! That's it," he exclaimed. "Tell me, Casperoon, are there many red squirrels in your woods?"

Casperoon failed to see the importance of squirrels but replied, "Yes, probably a thousand or so. They are our brave Red Squirrel Cavalry. They fight alongside the wild boar and badgers."

"Wild boar and badgers!" repeated Peter and he laughed again. "My dear old friend, I have it! We WILL stop this destruction of your home because these animals are *protected* by kind and thoughtful *Who Mans*. It is one of the better laws of our world. Your animal friends are quite rare, you see, and so we can get the police to help us, no less. Come on. We have much to do. Jump into my satchel."

And that is exactly what Casperoon and Glidestar did.

Back at the forest, the lazy and horrible Mr. Williams was by now barking orders from his car to his team of 20 men who had now arrived for work. He told them to get the tools from the shed and cut down another 100 trees today at least – the bigger the better! At first, the men complained about having to go through the gooey, muddy bog but, as Mr. Williams paid them very well, they agreed to try.

The men first tried to run across the bog, but then had to slow to a walk, and then to a crawl before they all came to a complete stop as they sunk up to their knees in the Goo-Trap. By the time they managed to drag themselves to the work shed, the stinky, sticky mud had sucked off their boots AND socks. YUCK! They were all very angry and quite smelly. Serves them right!

Finally, they grabbed their cutting tools and made their way very slowly across the mud trench again. However, unbeknown to the naughty *Who Mans*, the *Slow Ones'* cousins had been hiding in the bog, waiting for this moment. But they were not earthworms – they were leeches!

"AAAAGGGHH!" screamed the men as the leeches latched onto their feet, their toes and their ankles.

The *Who Mans* tried frantically to remove the leeches. As they lashed out at the leeches, Grouchy, who was standing on Willoughby's head, gave the order, "CHARGE!" He raced ahead of the armies of wild boar, badgers, bats, and hornets. At his side rode Scottlee 'Bulldog' Bashem with his Red Squirrel Cavalry right behind him. Bulldog was swinging a prickly horse chestnut on a small chain, ready to throw it. The *Who Mans* heard the stampede and fear engulfed them as they saw the unbelievable sight of thousands of wild animals and millions of insects charging and flying right towards them. They screamed again, this time like a bunch of scared young children. "MUMMY," one shouted, "HELP, HELP!"

As Grouchy charged with Willoughby, he whispered magic words to the young stinging nettles and prickly thorn bushes. The plants grew lightning fast and full, surrounding the now trapped *Who Mans*.

One *Who Man* managed to break free of the mud but then felt the sharp pain in his bottom as Bulldog's horse chestnut weapon hit its target.

"OOWWWW! THAT REALLY REALLY HURT," he cried. Then he tripped over some of the other *Who Mans* who were desperately trying to escape, screaming wildly, "MUMMY, HELP! THIS PLACE IS CURSED!" Then they all tumbled into the stinging nettles and sharp thorn bushes that had suddenly appeared from nowhere. "OUCHY! OUCH! OWW!"

It was complete pandemonium. The sharp thorns ripped the *Who*

Mans' clothes to shreds. They were now all stripped down to their underpants and were being stung all over by the nettles and the hornets. "PLEASE! SOMEONE! SAVE US!"

In desperation, they ran to their horseless carriages to speed away, but the wild boar, with their armour-plated tusks, had punctured all the tyres! Those smoky carriages were going nowhere! They would have to run for their lives all the way back to the City of Castles. The woodcutters ran straight past Mr. Williams, who had by now locked himself in his fancy carriage. The flying bats scooped up the itchy, sticky, stink bombs from carts pulled by the galloping badgers and then dropped them on the fleeing *Who Mans*.

"THIS PLACE IS CURSED! CURSED!" they screamed. Even the sacred trees joined in, tripping the fleeing *Who Mans* with their roots. The trees whispered together, "And don't come back, WHO MANS! DON'T COME BACK!"

The *Leaf Painters* were victorious. Everyone cheered and danced with joy! Grouchy even led the dance with Willoughby. Did you know wild boar can boogie? Everyone was so overjoyed they had not noticed that Mr. Williams had been watching them from his car. He could not believe his own eyes. Animals wearing armour? Tiny people flying around in capes? This place was indeed cursed!

He snuck out of his car, or rather slid out of his car, grabbed his shotgun, and was now aiming it straight at the obvious leader, Grouchy Gobman.

Tigerbella's sharp eyes had seen the danger her master was in and, quick as a flash, she and Zakia dived down from the sky towards the horrible *Who Man*. She gave a piercing battle cry and, upon hearing her, Mr. Williams turned the gun skywards and fired.

BANG! BANG!

The girl and the bat fell heavily to the ground.

There was complete silence. Tigerbella and Zakia were motionless. Grouchy raced over to them. In his head, all he could hear were the wise words of Winceyfloss, who had said *Who Mans* could not be beaten in a war. Now they had hurt his darling Tigerbella. Why had they not listened?

He was panting hard by the time he reached Tigerbella. She did not move. He feared the worst. He held her in his arms and cried like he had never cried before. Zakia had recovered and now joined him and began to lick her brave rider's forehead. But then, Grouchy felt the girl wriggle a little bit, and then giggle a lot. "Stop it, Zakia. STOP IT!"

Tigerbella was alive. Grouchy was overjoyed! Gingerly, Tigerbella got to her feet. Everyone was just about to cheer again when, suddenly, the giant Mr. Williams towered over Grouchy and Tigerbella. He had a very nasty grin on his ugly round face.

"Now, you strange little pests, I will feed you to my cats." He managed to bend over, which was not easy for him because his tummy hit the floor first. He was just about to pick them up when a loud sound filled the forest.

NEE NAH! NEE NAH!

The *Leaf Painters* watched in astonishment as the horseless electric carriages with flashing blue lights surrounded the horrible *Who Man*. And *who* was standing right on top of the flashing light? That's right. Good old Casperoon Eartheater, and he had the biggest of smiles on his face. This time, the *Leaf Painters* had truly won the war against the naughtiest of the *Who Mans*.

"HOORAY FOR CASPEROON THE ELDER. HOORAY FOR US ALL."

Nearly the Very End

The police put Mr. Williams in jail for a very long time for breaking many laws and being, well, truly horrible. They did not believe his claims about the tiny little flying folk who had by now retreated into the forest. The sacred forest and their rare animals were given special protection by very wise and good *Who Mans*.

Grouchy planted new strong trees to replace the ones lost and soon everything was as it should be. Peter, to this day, still does not tell anyone about the *Leaf Painters*. Apart from me, that is, and he said that I should only speak about them to **good** *Who Mans*, which is why I have now told you. Well, you are a kind and **good** *Who Man* – aren't you?

Truly the End

Now you know many secrets about the world *Outside*. See how many trees you can name when you leave the world *Inside* for your very own exciting adventure.

Perhaps one day you find your new friends using the secret map. Now, wouldn't that be fun?

Dear Friend,

Whilst you were reading this book, Casperoon came to see me. He has decreed that as you are a good *Who Man*, I can share more secrets and adventures with you.

But first, the *Leaf Painters* need my help to save their sacred woods again. Trees are dying from a mysterious disease and Casperoon thinks it has something to do with another naughty *Who Man*.

I must leave you now to go and see what it is all about. I will report back to you as soon as I can. Until then, do care for the trees and *Leaf Painters* near your home...... just outside your window.

Yours Truly

Peter

P.S.

Do share these secrets with your other good *Who Mans*. We may need their help too!

To learn more about the author and further adventures do visit
www.gjbunceauthor.com

Printed in Great Britain
by Amazon

16576050R00066